Marie Isaac

Big Dog and Brown Duck

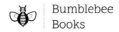

Bumblebee
Books

Olympia Publishers
London

BUMBLEBEE PAPERBACK EDITION
Copyright © Marie Isaac 2023

A CIP catalogue record for this title is
available from the British Library.

ISBN: 978-1-83934-782-5

Bumblebee Books is an imprint of
Olympia Publishers.

First Published in 2023

Bumblebee Books
Tallis House
2 Tallis Street
London
EC4Y 0AB

Printed in Great Britain

Dedication

This book is dedicated to the ever-inspiring Indy, Finn and Cael.

Big Dog and Brown Duck went out for a walk.

Big Dog was the loud one, how he liked to talk!

Brown Duck, she was quieter, with not much to say,

So he talked and she listened; they went on that way.

"I've walked down this path four or five times before,
With my great friend, the Royal Prince Mungo Lightpaw.
Such an elegant walker, so wonderfully bred,
And such interesting stories to tell," Big Dog said.

"Hurry up, won't you, Duck? You're dragging your feet.

If I move any slower, I might fall asleep!

Come on! Get a move on! Please don't be a bore,

Or I shan't go out walking with you anymore!"

Brown Duck hurried up and she lessened the gap,
But it wasn't enough, and he didn't like that.
Big Dog marched along, proudly yapping away.
As he boasted, she listened; they went on that way.

"What good are two legs, when you should have four?
It's obvious you can go faster with more.
You shuffle, you dawdle, you loiter, you creep.
I can race, I can scamper, I frolic, I leap!"

Brown Duck waddled on, hearing all that he said,
But she kept her beak shut, and just watched as he led.
She felt a bit useless compared to Big Dog,
And she tried to keep up by attempting to jog.

How he laughed at the sight of poor little Brown Duck,
Waddling faster but having no luck.
"Silly Duck! It's no use, you're no good, can't you see?
You'll never be able to keep up with me!"

He ran down the lane leaving Brown Duck behind,

He cared not a bit that he'd been so unkind.

He chortled and chuckled and strutted about.

"I'm the best, I'm the fastest, of that there's no doubt!"

"I'll prove it! I'll prove that you're no match for me –
Come on, Duck! Let's race to that sycamore tree!"
Brown Duck had enough now, of feeling so bad.
Anger took over and wiped out the sad.

Big Dog gave a grin and said, "One, two, three, GO!"
He was off like a shot chanting, "I told you so!"

Duck flapped and she ran, and she ran and she flapped;
Dog's mouth opened wide, and he stopped in his tracks.

Duck's feet left the ground and she flew gracefully,
Landing on top of the sycamore tree.

And reaching the tree, Dog sat and he glared,

"That's not fair! That's cheating!" he madly declared.

Still Duck was silent, no words did she say.

She just dropped him a parcel and then flew away.

About the Author

Marie Isaac is a great lover of animals and English, although her heart belongs to Scotland. She currently lives in the Staffordshire countryside with her partner, two dogs and two cats, and is always on the look out for a snail or two.